This edition published in 2020 in association with Crane Press

First published in 2015
Rockpool Children's Books Ltd.
Albury Court, Albury, Thame
OX9 2LP, United Kingdom

ISBN 978-1-906081-78-2 (Paperback)

Printed in China

Stuart Trotter

Big Bully
Hippo

Hippo looked out
of his window and said,
"What a lovely day for a walk."

Hippo splashed his way
through the water.

"Out of my way,"
he said rudely.

"What a big bully Hippo,"
said Duck.

"What a big bully Hippo,"
said the Fish.

Big Bully Hippo
hadn't gone far when...

"Give me a ride,"
snapped
Big Bully Hippo.

"Say please,"
said Crocodile.

But Big Bully Hippo
didn't and he squashed
Crocodile's bike.

"What a big bully
Hippo,"
snarled Crocodile.
"He didn't even
say sorry."

"Give me a drink,"
roared Big Bully Hippo.

"Say please,"
said Lion.

But Big Bully Hippo
didn't and he drank all
of Lion's drink.
**"What a big bully
Hippo,"** said Lion.

**"He didn't
even
say thank
you."**

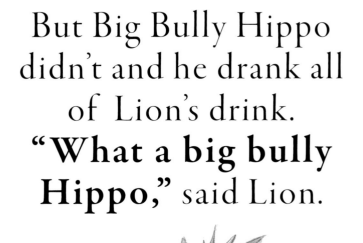

"Give me a balloon,"
shouted
Big Bully Hippo.

"Say please,"
said mommy
Baboon.

But he didn't,
and he
poked baby
Baboon's balloon
with his stick!

"**Boo-hoo,**" blubbed baby Baboon. "**He didn't even say sorry,**" said mommy Baboon.

POP!

POP!

POP!

"Give me a kick
of that ball."
boomed
Big Bully Hippo.

"I wouldn't kick
that if I were you,"
said Meerkat.

"**Buzzzzz,**"
buzzed the bees.
They were very
angry.

"Get the bees off me!"
yelped
Big Bully Hippo.

"Say please,"
said Elephant.

"Please!"
yelled
Big Bully Hippo

Elephant took
a big breath and...

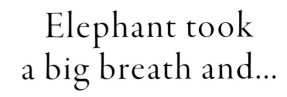

...blev

So Big Bully Hippo
had said,
"Please."
And he had said,
"Thank you."

...he bees away!

And to all the other animals, he said, **"Sorry."**

Big Bully Hippo had seen the error of his ways
and he became...

"Good morning."

...a perfectly polite Hippo.